DRAWING
SERGE PELLÉ

SCRIPT
SYLVAIN RUNBERG

ORBITAL

1. SCARS

9th CINEBOOK
The 9th Art Publisher

Original title: Orbital 1 – Cicatrices

Original edition: © Dupuis, 2006
by Runberg & Pellé
www.dupuis.com
All rights reserved

English translation: © 2009 Cinebook Ltd

Translator: Jerome Saincantin
Lettering and text layout: Imadjinn
Printed in Spain by Just Colour Graphic

This edition first published in Great Britain in 2009 by
Cinebook Ltd
56 Beech Avenue
Canterbury, Kent
CT4 7TA
www.cinebook.com

A CIP catalogue record for this book
is available from the British Library

ISBN 978-1-905460-89-2

9th CINEBOOK
The 9th Art Publisher

I'VE GOT A BAD FEELING ABOUT THIS REFERENDUM!

IF THE "YESES" WIN, WHAT'S GOING TO HAPPEN TO US?

QUIT WORRYING! WE'LL FINALLY HAVE ACCESS TO REAL INTERSTELLAR TRAVEL! ACTUALLY, MY LITTLE GIRL TALKS OF NOTHING ELSE!

YEAH, I DON'T KNOW...

I MEAN, THERE ARE ALREADY MORE THAN 500 RACES IN THAT CONFEDERATION!

781 EXACTLY. MY KID CAN'T STOP RAVING ABOUT THAT EITHER!

SO YOU'RE GOING TO VOTE YES?

THAT'S FOR SURE! IT'S THE ISOS' VIOLENCE THAT SCARES ME, NOT THE CONFEDERATION'S ALIENS. BESIDES, IF I VOTE NO, MY DAUGHTER WILL BLOW A GASKET ON ME!

MY RESPECTS, COLONEL ULRICH!

GOOD EVENING, SERGEANT...

HERE WE ARE, CHILDREN: AND, AS PROMISED, WITH AN UNBEATABLE VIEW OVER THE DOME WHERE THE CONVENTION IS TAKING PLACE!

THANKS, HECTOR! IT WAS REALLY COOL OF YOU TO BRING US HERE!

ALL THIS FOR THAT STINKING CONFEDERATION! IF MOM AND DAD SAW US, THEY'D BE FURIOUS, CALEB!

BUT IT'S US WHO ARE GOING TO WATCH THEM, KRISTINA! THE LAST PRO-CONFEDERATE MEETING BEFORE THE VOTE, AND IN OUR TOWN ON TOP OF IT. WE COULDN'T MISS THAT!

YOUR BROTHER'S RIGHT, YOU KNOW. THERE ARE OVER 120,000 PEOPLE OVER THERE WHO CAME FROM ALL OVER THE WORLD TO SUPPORT THE YESES!

AND IT'S OUR PARENTS WHO HAVE ORGANISED THIS CONVENTION, AFTER ALL!

EXACTLY, AND THEY HAD FORBIDDEN US FROM COMING NEAR THE DOME TODAY! DAD THINKS THAT SOME IGOS MIGHT WANT TO TRY SOMETHING BAD FOR THE OCCASION!

LISTEN KRISTINA, YOU'RE SAFE HERE, AND THAT'S WHY I AGREED TO TAKE YOU WITH ME. AND IF YOUR PARENTS GIVE YOU ANY TROUBLE, I'LL TAKE FULL RESPONSIBILITY FOR YOUR PRESENCE HERE, OK?

YOUR FATHER AND I MET WHEN WE WERE BARELY OLD ENOUGH TO SPEAK, SO I'LL KNOW HOW TO HANDLE IT, DON'T WORRY!

HMM...

I'LL LEAVE YOU TO YOUR WATCHING, AND IF YOU NEED ANYTHING, GIVE ME A SHOUT!

BRILLIANT! THIS IS JUST GREAT!

LADIES AND GENTLEMEN, AS THE MAYOR OF PRAGUE, IT IS WITH GREAT PLEASURE THAT I WELCOME YOU, ON THIS 24TH OF MAY 2278, TO THE LAST INTERNATIONAL CONFERENCE IN FAVOUR OF A CONFEDERATE YES!

4

BUT I WILL GIVE THE FLOOR TO THE ORGANISERS OF THIS EVENT, PAVEL SWANY AND IVANKA NAJMAN, HUSBAND AND WIFE, RENOWNED LINGUIST AND ASTROPHYSICIST, CITIZENS OF PRAGUE, AND ABOVE ALL, ARDENT PROPONENTS OF EARTH'S INTEGRATION!

THANK YOU, MISTER MAYOR! KNOW FIRST THAT WE ARE HAPPY TO SEE YOU ALL HERE, AND THIS DESPITE THE VIOLENCE THAT HAS DISRUPTED THIS WORLDWIDE CAMPAIGN...

THIS CAMPAIGN THROUGH WHICH WE WILL BE ABLE TO DECIDE IF MANKIND SHOULD BE PART OF THIS GREAT CONFEDERATION THAT IS OPENING ITS ARMS TO US!

I WILL ASK YOU TO GIVE A TRIUMPHANT WELCOME TO OUR FRIEND TWALIAN TOOT, WHO CAME HERE TO REPRESENT THE 781 RACES THAT MAKE UP THE CONFEDERATION! HIS PRESENCE FORETELLS THE COMING HARMONY THAT WILL LINK OUR SPECIES WITH THIS MULTI-CIVILISATIONAL BODY, WHICH IS MORE THAN 8,000 YEARS OLD!

HE IS THE SYMBOL OF THIS FUTURE FROM WHICH WE COULD EMERGE GREATER!

PARDON ME COLONEL ULRICH, BUT WHAT ARE THESE KIDS DOING WITH US?

THESE ARE PAVEL SWANY'S CHILDREN, SERGEANT. THE BOY ASKED ME IF HE COULD COME WATCH THE CONFERENCE FROM ONE OF OUR OBSERVATION POSTS, AND I THOUGHT IT BETTER TO SAY YES...

KNOWING HIM, HE'D HAVE TRIED TO COME ON HIS OWN ANYWAY...

SO, BETTER TO HAVE HIM AT MY SIDE!

WITH THESE INFRA-RED GOGGLES WE'LL BE ABLE TO SEE WHAT'S GOING ON INSIDE THE DOME AS IF WE WERE THERE! AND WITH THESE MICRO-SENSORS WE'LL GET REAL-TIME TRANSLATION! IT'S A CONFEDERATE DIPLOMAT WHO GAVE THEM TO DAD!

WHY? THEY EVEN SPEAK "CONFEDERATE" IN THERE?

DOES "SHINDAR" RING A BELL TO YOU?

YOU'RE SO DUMB! IT'S NOT RUSSIAN, IT'S HINDI!

THE NEW WORLD LANGUAGE? A MIX OF ARAB, ENGLISH, CHINESE AND RUSSIAN, RIGHT?

AND ONCE UNITED, WE WILL DEFEAT THE ISOLATIONISTS' EXTREMISM!

HEY... THERE WE GO! I SEE THEM! IT'S DAD TALKING NOW... WE MUST HAVE MISSED MOM'S SPEECH. MIND YOU, IT SEEMS THAT THEY LIKE WHAT HE HAS TO SAY!

EMBRACING THE CONFEDERATION WILL BRING ABOUT THE DAWN OF MAN!

HEY, GUYS, MY WAVE DEFRACTOR WON'T BE ABLE TO JAM THE BUILDING'S SECURITY SYSTEMS FOR MUCH LONGER!

DON'T SWEAT IT—ANOTHER THREE CONNECTORS AND WE'RE DONE!

THERE! WE'VE GOT THREE MINUTES TO SCRAM BEFORE THE OTHER MORONS EAT ELEMENTAL PARTICLES!

THANKS AGAIN FOR THE APARTMENT! WITH THE VIEW YOU HAD, IT WOULD HAVE BEEN A PITY NOT TO MAKE THE MOST OF IT!

I WANT TO GO BACK DOWN, CALEB! I DON'T WANT TO END UP ALL SOAKED!

KRIS! WE'RE LIVING A KEY MOMENT IN HISTORY AND YOU'RE WORRIED ABOUT THE RAIN?

YOU COULD HAVE A LITTLE MORE RESPECT FOR THE CAUSE OUR PARENTS ARE FIGHTING FOR, KRISTINA!

STOP ANNOYING ME WITH YOUR STINKING POLITICS! I DIDN'T ASK FOR ANY OF THIS!

I DON'T GIVE A DAMN ABOUT THAT REFERENDUM AND I WANT TO GET THE HELL OUT OF HERE!

LOOK OVER THERE!

EVERYTHING IN PLACE?

CLAC

PERFECTLY!

WHAT ON EARTH IS THAT?!

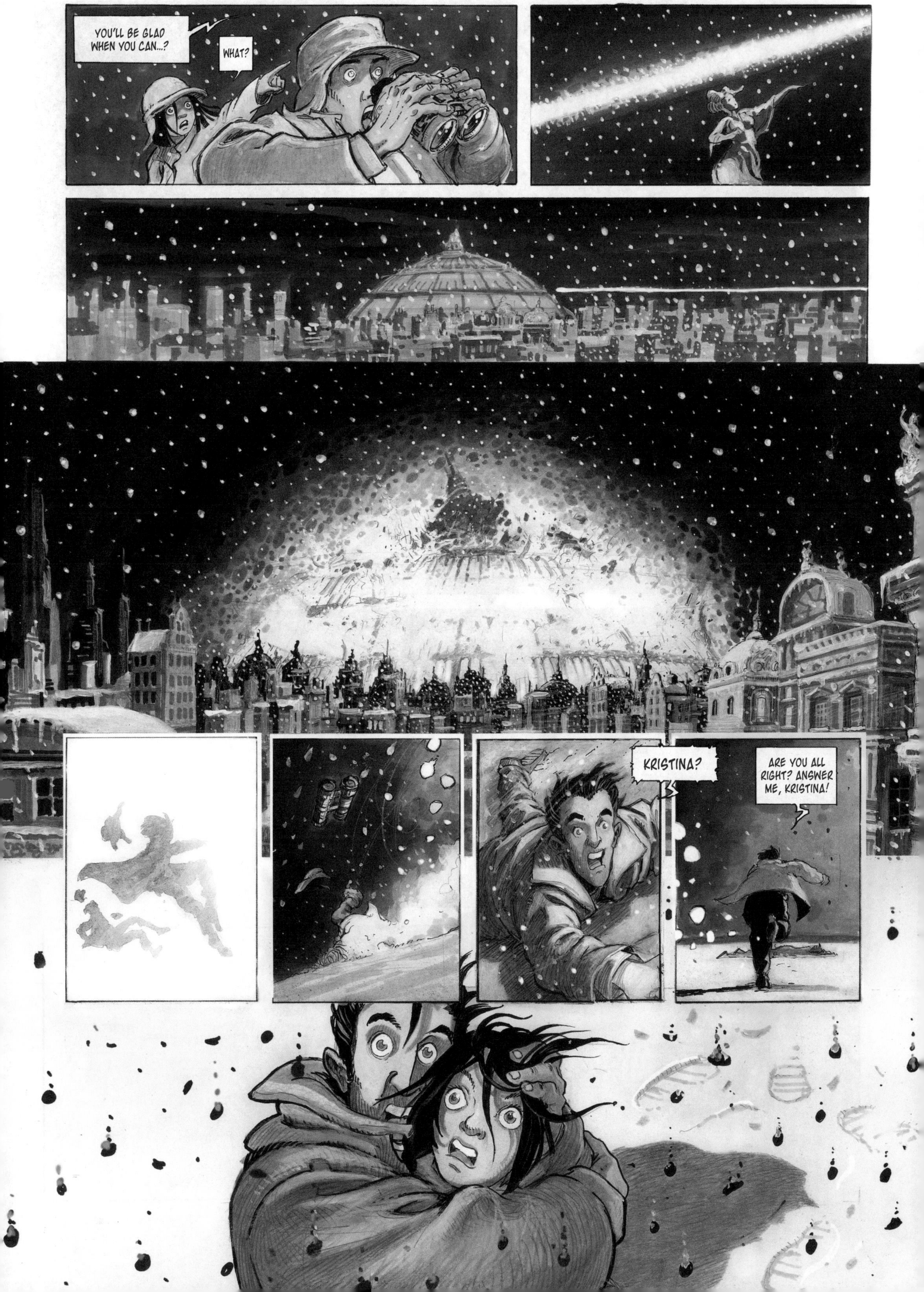
YOU'LL BE GLAD WHEN YOU CAN...?
WHAT?
KRISTINA?
ARE YOU ALL RIGHT? ANSWER ME, KRISTINA!

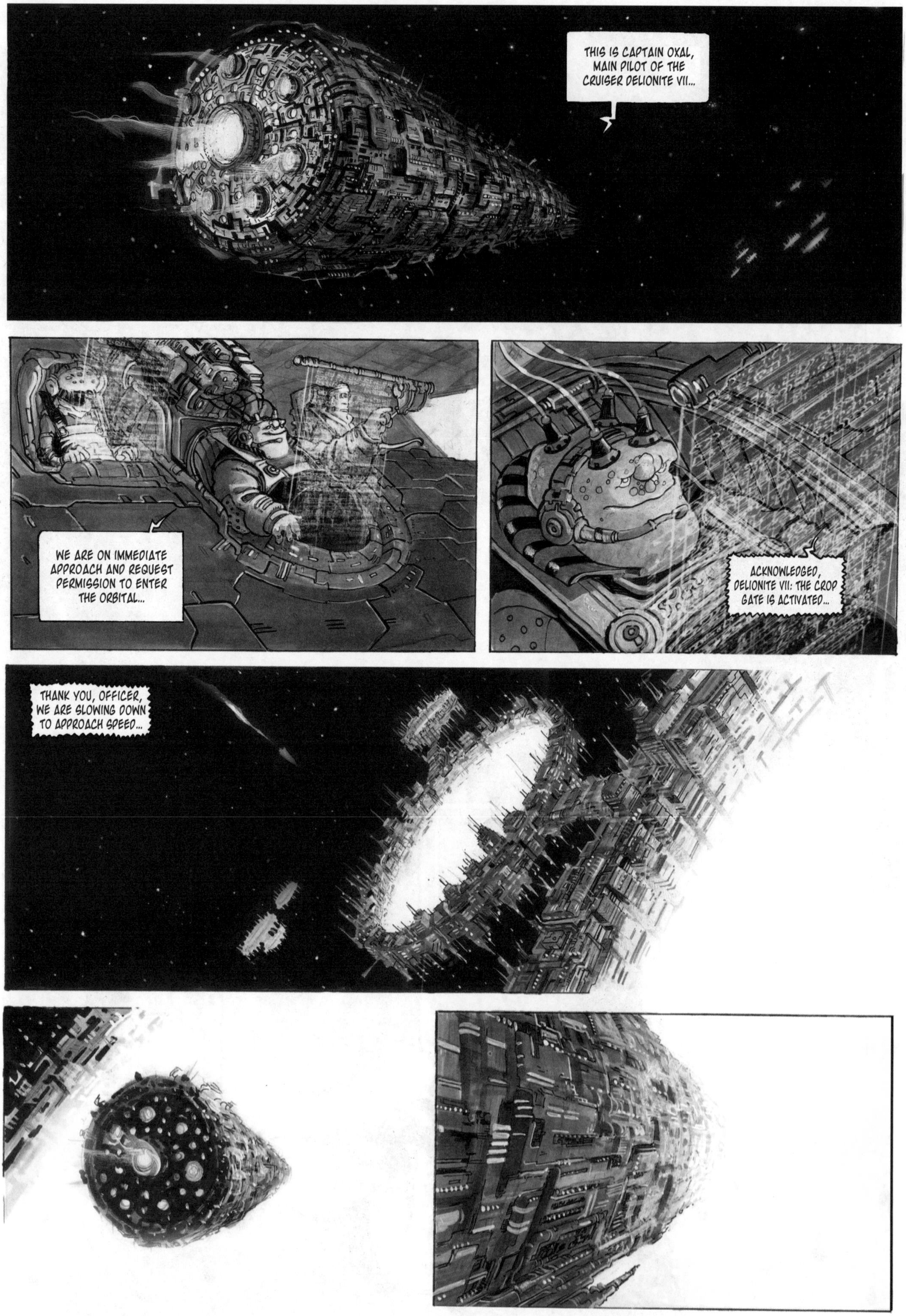

THIS IS CAPTAIN OXAL, MAIN PILOT OF THE CRUISER DELIONITE VII...
WE ARE ON IMMEDIATE APPROACH AND REQUEST PERMISSION TO ENTER THE ORBITAL...
ACKNOWLEDGED, DELIONITE VII: THE CROP GATE IS ACTIVATED...
THANK YOU, OFFICER, WE ARE SLOWING DOWN TO APPROACH SPEED...

COMMANDER KUSIO, I HAVE RECEIVED CONFIRMATION THAT THE DELIONITE VII HAS ARRIVED DOCK 673...

EXCELLENT NEWS, LIEUTENANT! TWO DAYS' DELAY BECAUSE OF A MERE MAGNETIC STORM. THAT'S UNHEARD OF!

OUR YOUNG RECRUITS CAME CLOSE TO MISSING THEIR OWN ENTRANCE INTO THE IDO!

CAPTAIN OXAL, WE ARE LOCKED IN STATI-GRAVITY...

THANK YOU, PILOT DIPIR! TO BE HONEST, I'M RATHER GLAD TO BRING THIS CRUISE TO A STOP... IN 20 YEARS OF STELLAR NAVIGATION, I'VE NEVER FACED SUCH A STORM!

THIS IS THE HATCH RESERVED FOR OFFICIALS, COMMANDER...

GOOD. I CAN'T WAIT TO GET MY NEW AGENTS!

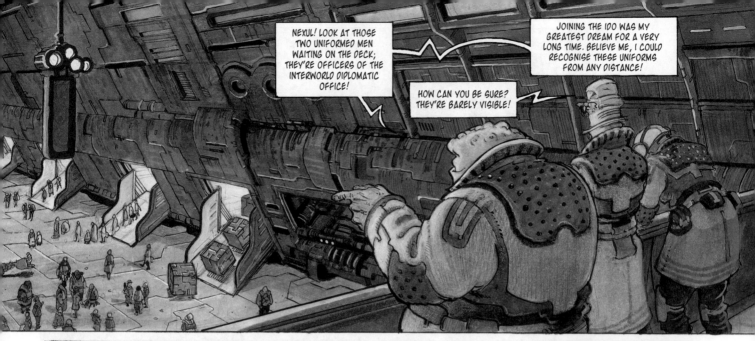

NEXUL! LOOK AT THOSE TWO UNIFORMED MEN WAITING ON THE DECK; THEY'RE OFFICERS OF THE INTERWORLD DIPLOMATIC OFFICE!

JOINING THE IDO WAS MY GREATEST DREAM FOR A VERY LONG TIME. BELIEVE ME, I COULD RECOGNISE THESE UNIFORMS FROM ANY DISTANCE!

HOW CAN YOU BE SURE? THEY'RE BARELY VISIBLE!

WELCOME TO YOU ALL! WE WERE STARTING TO WORRY ABOUT YOU!

AFTER I WAS REFUSED DURING THEIR PRE-SELECTIONS, I FELL BACK ONTO A PILOT CAREER...

AND RIGHT THERE I'M SURE WE HAVE AMONG OUR PASSENGERS A NEW CLASS COMING TO JOIN THE OFFICE: THEIR GRADUATION CEREMONIES ALWAYS TAKE PLACE ON ORBITAL!

AGENT DJENO-HIIAS IS HERE; SO IS AGENT SHARLEK...

HOWEVER, ONE OF YOU IS STILL MISSING!

WHO WOULD THAT BE, LIEUTENANT TEONIS?

I AM CALEB SWANY!

AGENT SWANY, A RECRUIT FROM...?

HERE I AM, LIEUTENANT, DON'T WORRY!

LET'S HURRY UP, THEN! YOUR FUTURE PARTNERS ARRIVED A WEEK AGO AND YOU'RE ALREADY TWO DAYS LATE ON THE PROGRAM.

THE PAIRING CEREMONY WILL TAKE PLACE IN LESS THAN FOUR HOURS. YOU'LL BARELY HAVE THE TIME TO GET READY!

PARDON ME, COMMANDER, BUT THERE IS SOMETHING I DO NOT UNDERSTAND...

?!

WAS THIS HUMAN SELECTED BY THE OFFICE AS A DIPLOMATIC AGENT? I THOUGHT THEY WERE STRICTLY FORBIDDEN FROM HOLDING SUCH POSITIONS SINCE THE SANDJARR WARS!

AGENT SHARLEK, IT IS NOT YOUR PLACE TO COMMENT ON THE SELECTIONS MADE BY YOUR NEW HIERARCHY! AND YES, I CAN CONFIRM THAT THIS HUMAN IS NOW PART OF THE IDO, JUST AS ANY ONE OF YOU!

BUT THAT'S INCONCEIVABLE! HOW COULD A HUMAN SUCCESSFULLY COMPLETE A DIPLOMATIC MISSION?!

THAT'S ENOUGH, SHARLEK! ONE MORE REMARK LIKE THIS ONE AND YOU'RE OUT! GET ON THAT SHUTTLE!

NOW!

PLEASE FORGIVE ME, COMMANDER...

LET'S GO! WE CAN'T WASTE ANY MORE TIME!

WE MUST GET TO THE IDO HEADQUARTERS AS QUICKLY AS POSSIBLE!

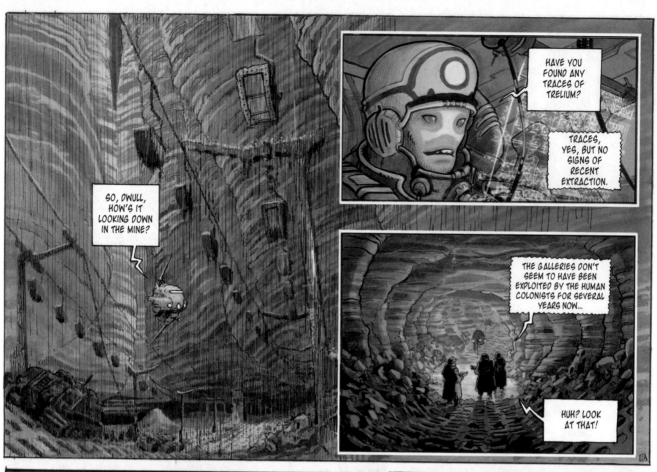

HAVE YOU FOUND ANY TRACES OF TRELIUM?

TRACES, YES, BUT NO SIGNS OF RECENT EXTRACTION.

SO, OWULL, HOW'S IT LOOKING DOWN IN THE MINE?

THE GALLERIES DON'T SEEM TO HAVE BEEN EXPLOITED BY THE HUMAN COLONISTS FOR SEVERAL YEARS NOW...

HUH? LOOK AT THAT!

THESE ARE STILVULL EGGS...

THESE ARTHROPODS FEED ON MINERAL WASTE. IT'S NO WONDER THEY SETTLED IN THESE MINES!

STILVULLS? I DIDN'T KNOW THOSE NASTY CRITTERS HAD SPREAD TO OUR SOLAR SYSTEM! DO YOU WANT TO HEAD BACK?

THAT WON'T BE NECESSARY, LIKO'D...

ADULT STILVULLS DIE WHEN THEY LAY THEIR EGGS, AND THESE LARVAE SEEM FRESH, SO THERE SHOULDN'T BE ANY DANGER...

WE GO ON!

WAIT! I'VE DETECTED A LARGE CAVE AT THE END OF THIS TUNNEL...

IT'S SURROUNDED BY METALLIC STRUCTURES, AS IF IT WAS OF ARTIFICIAL NATURE. THAT'S NOT NORMAL: THAT DEEP, THERE SHOULD ONLY BE OLD POCKETS OF TRELIUM...

RIGHT, WE'LL JUST CHECK OUT WHAT IT IS, THEN HEAD BACK UP...

I DON'T REALLY WANT TO STICK AROUND THESE ROTTEN CAVES FOR TOO LONG!

14

FOR THOSE WHO MAY NOT YET KNOW WHO I AM, ALLOW ME TO INTRODUCE MYSELF...

MY NAME IS EVONA TOOT, THE PRIME DIGNITARY PRESIDING OVER THE IDO DIRECTORATE...

I HOPE THAT, TOGETHER, WE WILL PERPETUATE THE NOBLE DUTY THAT HAS BEEN ENTRUSTED TO THIS OFFICE FOR OVER 30 CENTURIES NOW...

PRESERVING PEACE AND UNDERSTANDING WITHIN OUR VAST CONFEDERATION, SOLELY BY DIPLOMATIC MEANS.

THE FIRST PAIR I WILL NOW NAME IS, FOR US, MEMBERS OF THE DIRECTORATE, OF PARTICULAR IMPORTANCE AS A SYMBOL...

THIS PAIR REPRESENTS THE SUPERIORITY OF THE VALUES OF PEACE OVER ALL FORMS OF DISAGREEMENT, THE VICTORY OF INTELLIGENCE OVER HATRED, OF RECONCILIATION OVER CONFLICT...

LET THE TWO AGENTS CALLED COME FORWARD AND TAKE THEIR VOWS OF ALLEGIANCE!

15

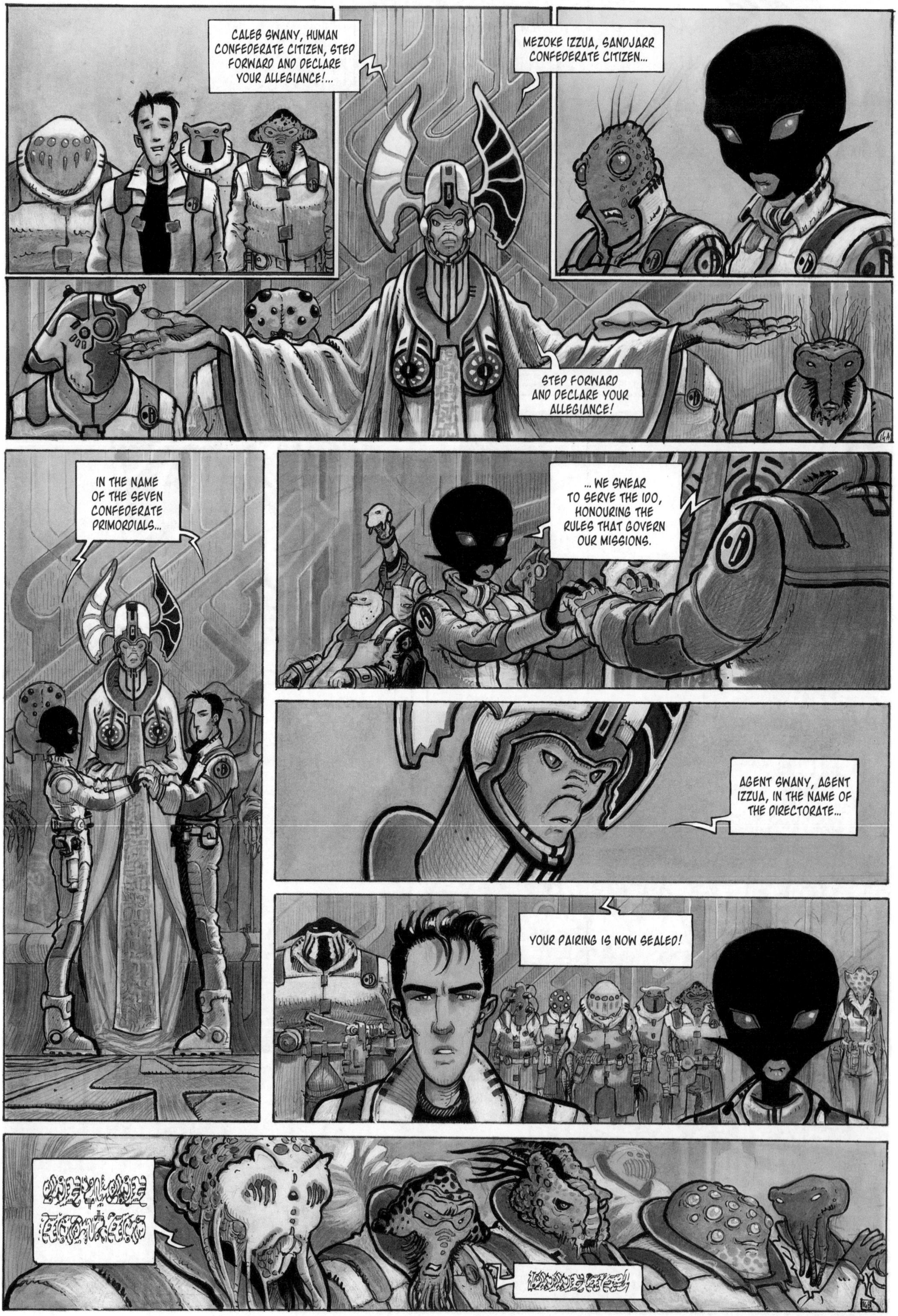
CALEB SWANY, HUMAN CONFEDERATE CITIZEN, STEP FORWARD AND DECLARE YOUR ALLEGIANCE!...
MEZOKE IZZUA, SANDJARR CONFEDERATE CITIZEN...
STEP FORWARD AND DECLARE YOUR ALLEGIANCE!
IN THE NAME OF THE SEVEN CONFEDERATE PRIMORDIALS...
... WE SWEAR TO SERVE THE IDO, HONOURING THE RULES THAT GOVERN OUR MISSIONS.
AGENT SWANY, AGENT IZZUA, IN THE NAME OF THE DIRECTORATE...
YOUR PAIRING IS NOW SEALED!

DO YOU BELIEVE YOU CAN FORCE YOUR WAY IN, DWULL?

IT'S A HATCH SEALED WITH A GENETIC CODE, BUT THE LEVEL OF SECURITY ISN'T SO HIGH THAT IT WILL CREATE ANY DIFFICULTIES FOR OUR DROID: WE'LL BE ABLE TO GET IN WITHOUT MUCH TROUBLE!

CLAC

THAT'S IT. THE HATCH IS OPENING!

WELL... WHAT'S BEHIND IT?

Tiiiii

IT'S JUST AS WE THOUGHT, LIKO'O!

DWULL! I HAVE ECHOES ON MY RADAR...

A DOZEN VEHICLES ARE HEADING STRAIGHT TOWARDS US!

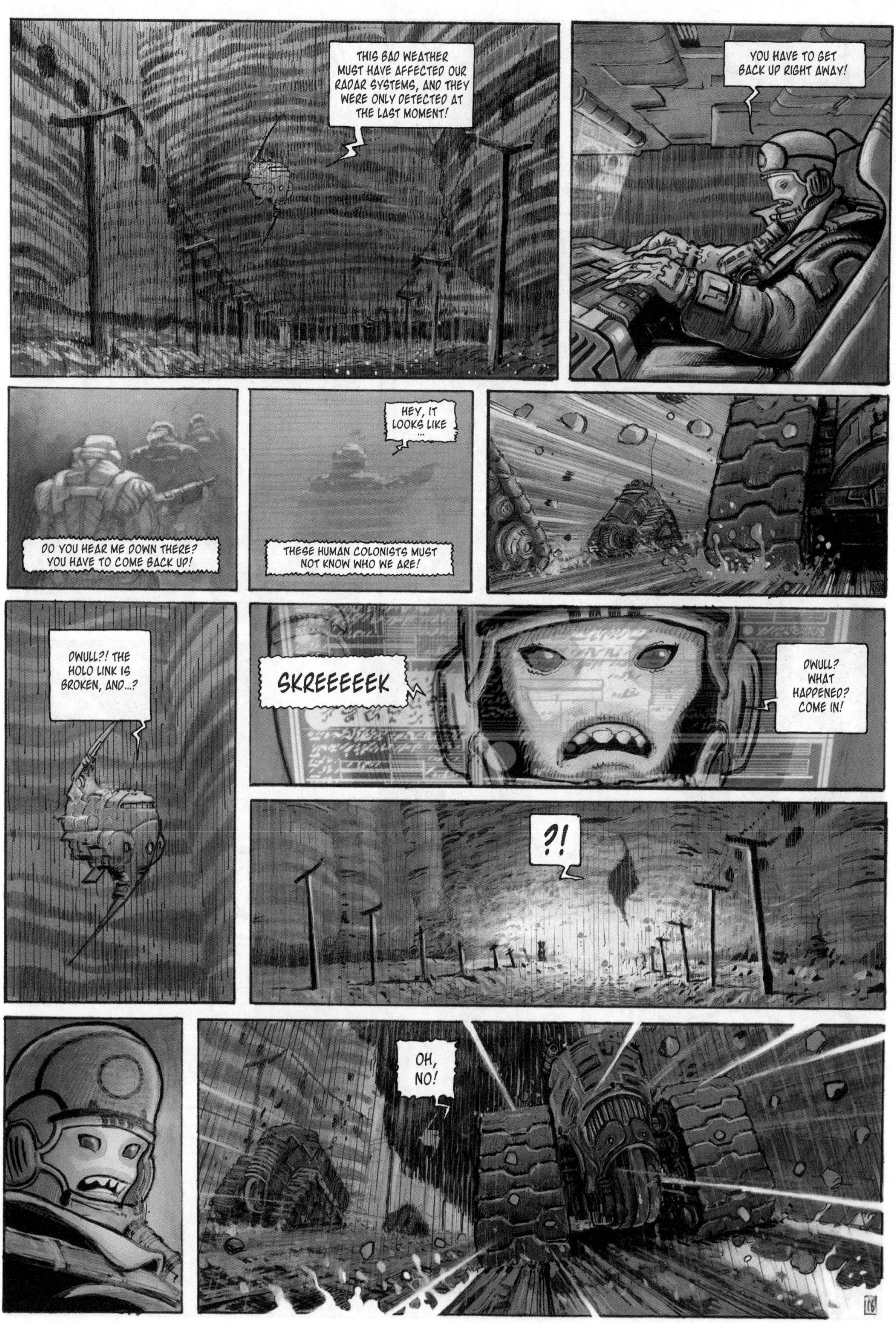
THIS BAD WEATHER MUST HAVE AFFECTED OUR RADAR SYSTEMS, AND THEY WERE ONLY DETECTED AT THE LAST MOMENT!
YOU HAVE TO GET BACK UP RIGHT AWAY!
DO YOU HEAR ME DOWN THERE? YOU HAVE TO COME BACK UP!
HEY, IT LOOKS LIKE ...
THESE HUMAN COLONISTS MUST NOT KNOW WHO WE ARE!
OWULL?! THE HOLO LINK IS BROKEN, AND...?
SKREEEEEK
OWULL? WHAT HAPPENED? COME IN!
?!
OH, NO!

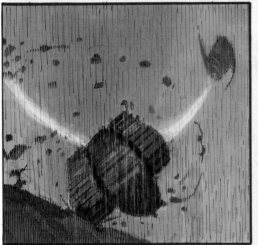

BLOODY ALIENS!

CEASE FIRE, PEETERS! STOP IT!

OUR COLONY IS GOING TO BE IN ENOUGH TROUBLE ALREADY...

NO NEED TO ADD TO IT BY SHOOTING DOWN A JÄVLOD SHIP!

PARTY DROID DESIGNATED T3-TYU-24. I AM BRINGING IN FRESH DISHES FOR THE RECEPTION IN HONOUR OF THE NEW PAIRS.

WE DID FIGURE IT WASN'T FOR US, DROID!

THE SCAN READS OK. YOU CAN GO IN.

THANK YOU!

TO THINK WE'VE BEEN ON DUTY FOR OVER SIX HOURS AND ALL WE GET IS ENERGY DRINKS!

IF YOU WANTED TO ENJOY THE RECEPTION, HUMAN, ALL YOU HAD TO DO WAS PASS THE 100 ADMISSION EXAMS...

AS A MATTER OF FACT, I HEAR THAT ONE OF YOUR PEOPLE JUST MANAGED THAT FEAT!

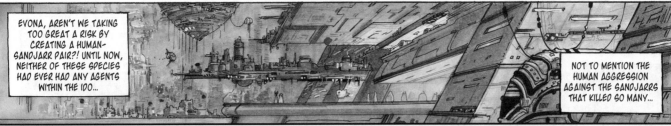

EVONA, AREN'T WE TAKING TOO GREAT A RISK BY CREATING A HUMAN-SANDJARR PAIR?! UNTIL NOW, NEITHER OF THESE SPECIES HAD EVER HAD ANY AGENTS WITHIN THE IDO...

NOT TO MENTION THE HUMAN AGGRESSION AGAINST THE SANDJARRS THAT KILLED SO MANY...

AFTER ALL, IT'S ONLY BEEN 15 YEARS SINCE THE ATTACK...

YOU KNOW, KLEOKALT, IT'S NOT ALWAYS BEST TO LET TIME HEAL ALL WOUNDS...

THE SANDJARRS WERE FEW IN NUMBERS BEFORE THAT WAR, AND THEY ALMOST DISAPPEARED COMPLETELY BECAUSE OF THE HUMANS...

THEY'RE A RARE PEOPLE WHO, DESPITE HAVING LONG BELONGED TO THE CONFEDERATION, HAVE ALWAYS STOOD APART FROM OUR MAIN POLITICAL INSTITUTIONS...

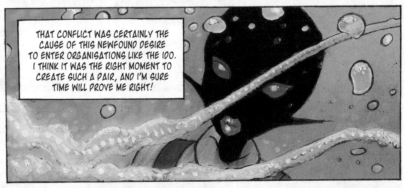

THAT CONFLICT WAS CERTAINLY THE CAUSE OF THIS NEWFOUND DESIRE TO ENTER ORGANISATIONS LIKE THE IDO. I THINK IT WAS THE RIGHT MOMENT TO CREATE SUCH A PAIR, AND I'M SURE TIME WILL PROVE ME RIGHT!

BY THE WAY, DID YOU KNOW THAT CALEB SWANY'S PARENTS WERE KILLED BY HUMANS HOSTILE TO THE CONFEDERATION?

THE BOMBING KILLED THOUSANDS. BY A STRANGE COINCIDENCE, THE AMBASSADOR WHO REPRESENTED THE CONFEDERATION WAS ONE OF MY COUSINIDEA...

IN A WAY, CALEB SWANY AND I SHARE A COMMON GRIEF.

CONGRATULATIONS ON YOUR PROMOTION, BUDDY! A HUMAN IN THE IDO: THAT'S A STEP UP FROM THE ROTTEN JOBS THE CONF'S USUALLY KEEP US DOING!

THANKS! JUST GOES TO SHOW, ANYTHING'S POSSIBLE, ISN'T IT?

ANYTHING'S POSSIBLE? I DON'T BELIEVE THAT JUST YET!

UNTIL NOW, A HUMAN ON ORBITAL COULD AT BEST MAKE BARMAN AND ORDER SOME DROIDS AROUND! OR MAYBE A JOB IN SECURITY FOR THE BRAWNIEST!

AND EVEN WITH WHAT HAPPENED TO YOU, I THINK IN THE END THAT AIN'T ABOUT TO CHANGE!

BESIDES, IT DOESN'T LOOK LIKE YOU'RE UNANIMOUSLY ACCEPTED BY YOUR NEW BUDDIES, RIGHT?

THEY'LL GET USED TO IT...

I HAVE A FEELING THAT YOU, ON THE OTHER HAND, TEND TO IGNORE THE ADVANTAGES OF OUR INTEGRATION.

THE EARTH HAS GREATLY BENEFITED FROM CONFEDERATE TECHNOLOGY: CENTURIES OF MANMADE POLLUTION SCRUBBED AWAY IN A FEW YEARS. THAT'S PROGRESS, ISN'T IT?

YEAH! WELL, IF IT WAS TO END UP A BUNCH OF TOILET-CLEANERS AND GOONS FOR THE MARTIANS, MAYBE WE WERE BETTER OFF IN OUR OWN CRAP!

AND I CAN'T STAND THE IDEA OF HAVING THEIR BLOODY TRANSLATOR IMPLANTS STUCK IN MY NOGGIN!

WELL, UNLESS IT'S TO CHAT UP SOME OF THEIR PRETTIES...

THAT'S YOUR PAIRING PARTNER CAMPING IN FRONT OF THE AQUARIUMS, ISN'T IT?

ERM...

'CAUSE, YOU SEE, AS MUCH AS I CAN'T STAND ALIENS IN GENERAL...

I'D REALLY LOVE TO CORNER YOURS IN PARTICULAR!

EVEN THOUGH THEY'RE DIVIDED INTO MALE AND FEMALE, THEIR PHYSICAL APPEARANCE IS OF NO HELP AT ALL IN IDENTIFYING THEIR GENDER.

TOO RANDOM.

ADMIT IT: IT'S CROSSED YOUR MIND, HEY, BUDDY?

YOU KNOW VERY LITTLE ABOUT THE SANDJARRS, FRIEND...

AND SINCE THEIR CULTURE DOESN'T PLACE ANY IMPORTANCE ON GENDER IN SOCIAL INTERACTIONS...

REVEALING THEIR TRUE SEXUAL NATURE TO NON-SANDJARRS IS CONSIDERED AN INFRINGEMENT ON THE INTEGRITY OF THEIR INDIVIDUALITY, A DEFAMATORY NONSENSE.

HANG ON, I DON'T GET IT... ARE YOU TELLING ME THAT YOUR ALIEN THERE IS ACTUALLY A GUY?...

I'M TELLING YOU THAT I HAVE NO IDEA...

AND THAT I'M NOT LIKELY TO KNOW ANYTIME SOON!

23

THIS WILL BE YOUR LAST TRAINING DURING THIS TRANSITIONAL PERIOD!

THE REST OF YOUR CLASSMATES HAVING RECEIVED THEIR FIRST MISSIONS WITHOUT HAVING HAD TO FACE IT...

I WILL ASK YOU TO VIEW THIS EXERCISE AS A PRIVILEGE!

THESE MAGNETOPODS WILL ALLOW YOU TO TEST YOUR REFLEXES IN RAPID MOVEMENT SITUATIONS.

THIS CORRIDOR WILL BE YOUR MISSION ZONE...

YOUR OBJECTIVE IS TO REACH THE OTHER END AS QUICKLY AS POSSIBLE, WHILE AVOIDING THE ANTI-G MINES THAT HAVE BEEN LAID ALONG ITS LENGTH...

THESE MINES ARE NONLETHAL, OF COURSE.

WE'VE BEEN ON ORBITAL THREE DAYS, MEZOKE, AND YOU HAVE YET TO SAY ONE WORD TO ME...

DURING TRAINING WE MIGHT BE ABLE TO MAKE DO. BUT ONCE WE'RE ON A MISSION, WE'LL HAVE TO COMMUNICATE!

VERY WELL.

I WON'T PUSH YOU.

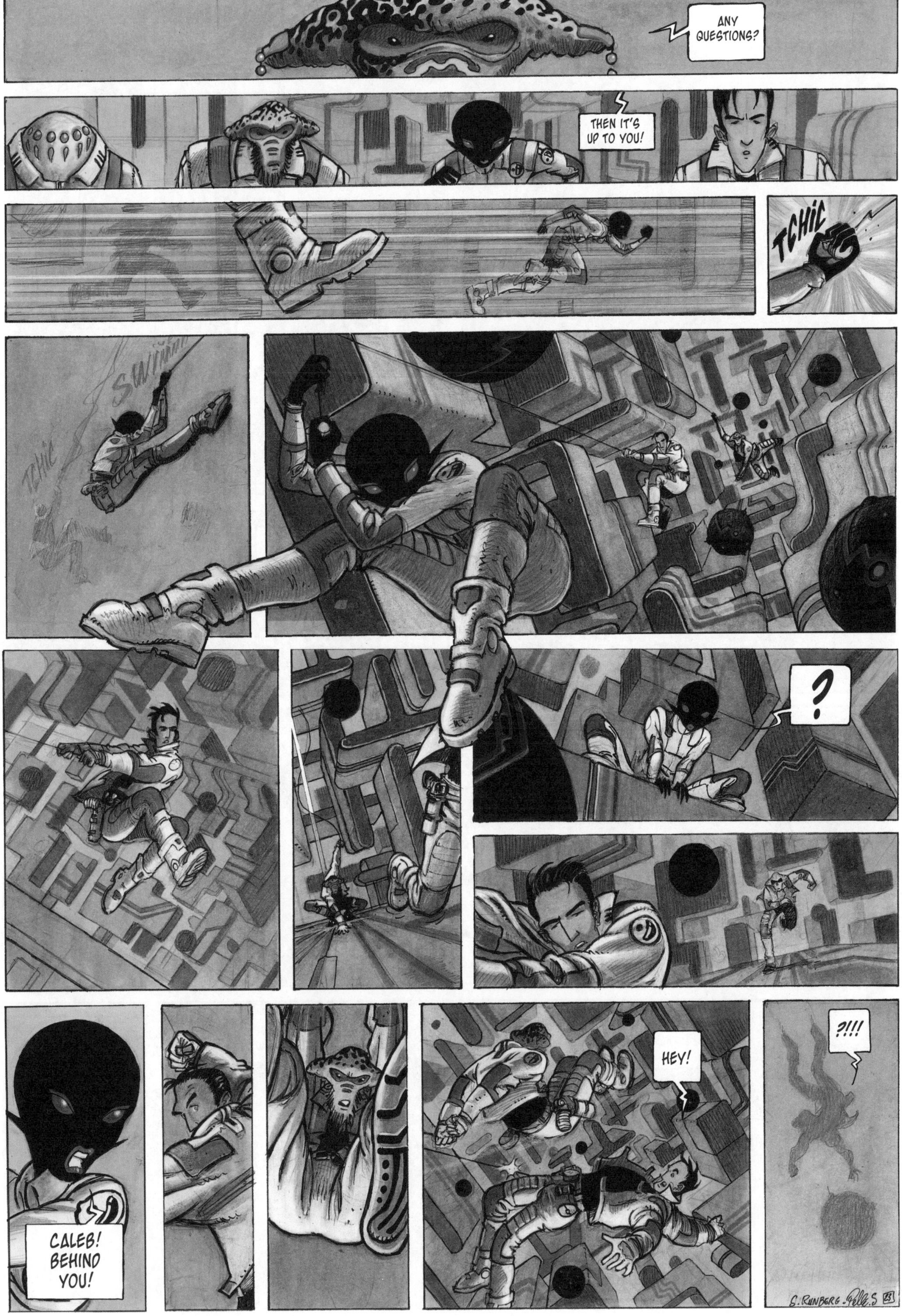
ANY QUESTIONS?
THEN IT'S UP TO YOU!
TCHIC
SWIIIIIII
TCHIC
?
CALEB! BEHIND YOU!
HEY!
?!!!
S. RUNBERG · PELLE.S 25

ARG!

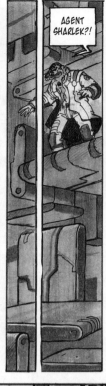

AGENT SHARLEK?!

PLOMG

HAVE YOU LOST YOUR MIND, SWANY?!

WHAT ARE YOU TALKING ABOUT?

I ASKED YOU TO COMPLETE A COURSE, NOT ASSAULT YOUR CLASSMATES!

HE'S THE ONE WHO CHARGED ME!

I ADVISE YOU TO WATCH YOUR TONE WITH ME!

YET HE IS CORRECT, INSTRUCTOR SHIRUIL!

SHARLEK ATTACKED HIM...

IT WAS I WHO ALERTED AGENT SWANY SO HE COULD EVADE!

HOW CAN YOU DEFEND THOSE WHO ATTACKED YOUR PEOPLE?!

HAVE YOU FORGOTTEN THAT A DIPLOMATIC AGENT MUST STAND TOGETHER WITH THOSE OF HIS STATION?

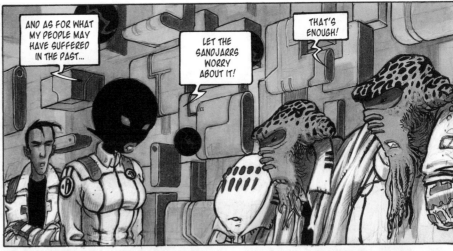

AND AS FOR WHAT MY PEOPLE MAY HAVE SUFFERED IN THE PAST...

LET THE SANDJARRS WORRY ABOUT IT!

THAT'S ENOUGH!

TRAINING IS POSTPONED AND I DON'T WANT TO HEAR ABOUT THIS INCIDENT AGAIN!

AND TO THINK THESE TERRAN PARASITES WEREN'T EVEN CAPABLE OF LEAVING THEIR SOLAR SYSTEM BEFORE THEY JOINED US!

I DON'T LIKE THEM ANY MORE THAN YOU DO, SHARLEK, BUT WE HAVE TO RESPECT THE CONFEDERATION'S DECISIONS...

THANK YOU FOR YOUR HELP, MEZOKE...

AGENTS IZZUA AND SWANY?

I AM COLONEL KARLUS DOMANN, 1ST TERRAN DIVISION OF THE CONFEDERATE ARMY.

THE DIRECTORATE ASKED ME TO GIVE YOU YOUR DIPLOMATIC HOLOCUBES.

ALL THE DATA REGARDING YOUR FIRST MISSION HAVE BEEN TRANSFERRED TO THEM, LOCKED FROM ACCESS UNTIL AFTER YOU HAVE LEFT ORBITAL, PER STANDARD PROCEDURE.

I WILL BE THE ONE IN CHARGE OF PROVIDING YOUR LOGISTICAL SUPPORT DURING THIS OPERATION. A STAR TRANSPORT IS ALREADY WAITING FOR US.

WE MUST TAKE OFF IN THREE HOURS AT THE MOST!

THIS IS THE ELITE COMMANDO "HOPE"... THESE MEN COME FROM THE BEST HUMAN UNITS OF THE CONFEDERATE ARMY...

THEY WILL BE UNDER MY DIRECT ORDERS AND WILL PROVIDE SECURITY FOR YOU DURING THIS MISSION!

HOW DOES AN IDO DIPLO-MATIC MISSION REQUIRE THE PRESENCE OF SUCH A COMBAT UNIT, COLONEL?

DON'T WORRY...

THEY'LL KNOW TO REMAIN IN THE BACK-GROUND AND WILL ONLY INTERVENE IF YOUR LIVES ARE THREATENED!

BUT I SUGGEST WE GET ONBOARD IF WE WANT TO KEEP TO OUR FLIGHT PLAN!

TO THINK THAT OVER 300 MILLION INDIVIDUALS LIVE BEHIND THESE CROP GATES...

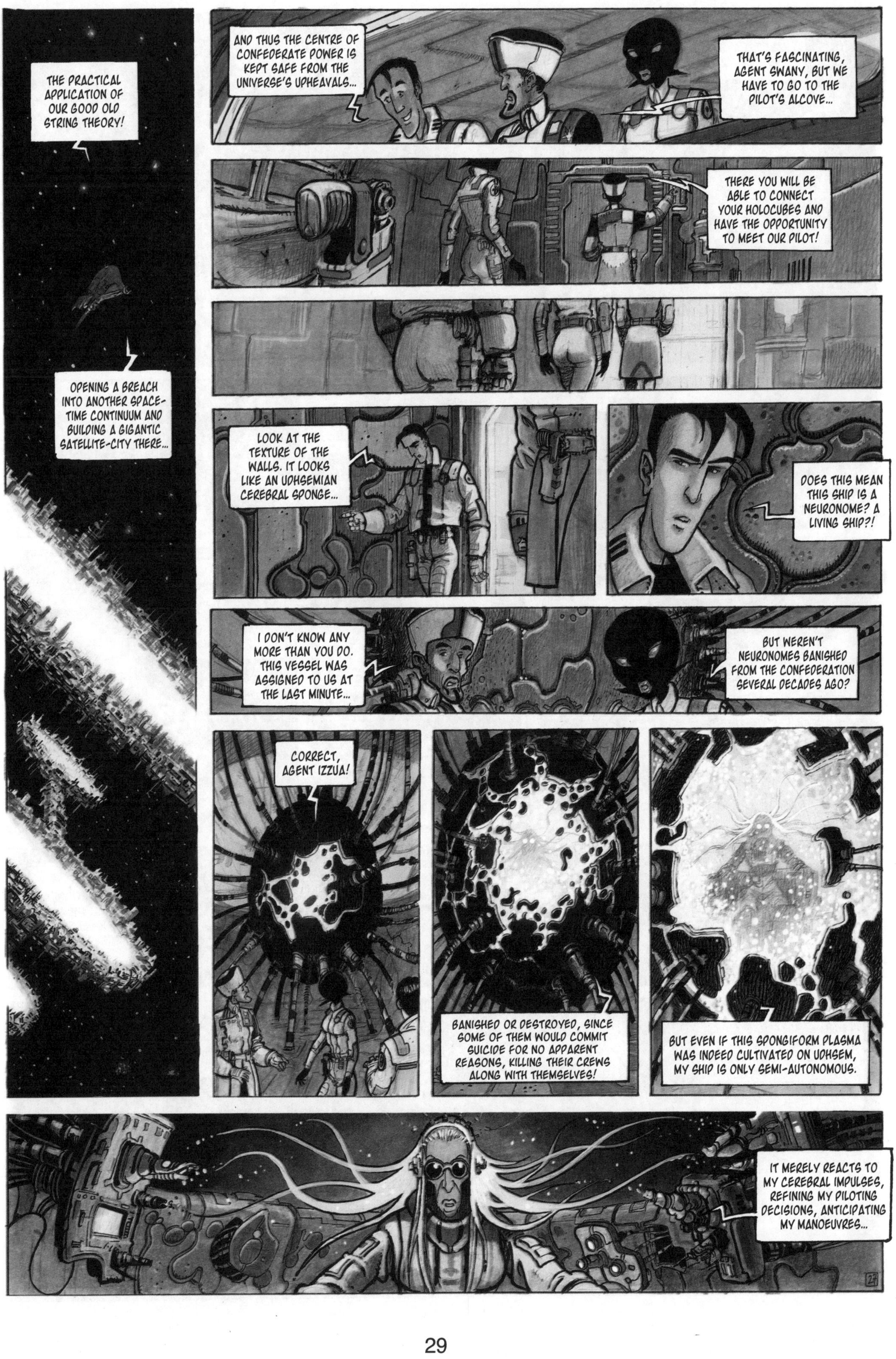
THE PRACTICAL APPLICATION OF OUR GOOD OLD STRING THEORY!
OPENING A BREACH INTO ANOTHER SPACE-TIME CONTINUUM AND BUILDING A GIGANTIC SATELLITE-CITY THERE...
AND THUS THE CENTRE OF CONFEDERATE POWER IS KEPT SAFE FROM THE UNIVERSE'S UPHEAVALS...
THAT'S FASCINATING, AGENT SWANY, BUT WE HAVE TO GO TO THE PILOT'S ALCOVE...
THERE YOU WILL BE ABLE TO CONNECT YOUR HOLOCUBES AND HAVE THE OPPORTUNITY TO MEET OUR PILOT!
LOOK AT THE TEXTURE OF THE WALLS. IT LOOKS LIKE AN UDHSEMIAN CEREBRAL SPONGE...
DOES THIS MEAN THIS SHIP IS A NEURONOME? A LIVING SHIP?!
I DON'T KNOW ANY MORE THAN YOU DO. THIS VESSEL WAS ASSIGNED TO US AT THE LAST MINUTE...
BUT WEREN'T NEURONOMES BANISHED FROM THE CONFEDERATION SEVERAL DECADES AGO?
CORRECT, AGENT IZZUA!
BANISHED OR DESTROYED, SINCE SOME OF THEM WOULD COMMIT SUICIDE FOR NO APPARENT REASONS, KILLING THEIR CREWS ALONG WITH THEMSELVES!
BUT EVEN IF THIS SPONGIFORM PLASMA WAS INDEED CULTIVATED ON UDHSEM, MY SHIP IS ONLY SEMI-AUTONOMOUS.
IT MERELY REACTS TO MY CEREBRAL IMPULSES, REFINING MY PILOTING DECISIONS, ANTICIPATING MY MANOEUVRES...
27

I NAMED IT ANGUS. JUST FOR FUN.

AND I AM NINA LIEBERT, STAR PILOT, AT YOUR SERVICE!

HOW CAN YOU BE A PILOT?

AT MY AGE?

SIMPLE...

I JOINED THE CONFEDERATE SYSTEM WELL BEFORE EARTH'S OFFICIAL ADMISSION!

YOU'RE AN EXTRACT, AREN'T YOU?

MMH... IT HAPPENED BACK IN THE SUMMER OF 2256: I WAS 30, I LIVED IN BERLIN AND I WAS BORED OUT OF MY SKULL!

SOME WELBU'RR SCIENTISTS WHO DISAGREED WITH THE CONFEDERATE POLICY PROHIBITING THE INTRODUCTION OF NON-MEMBER BEINGS CONTACTED ME...

LIKE THOUSANDS OF OTHER HUMANS BEFORE ME, I WENT WITH THEM, LEAVING GOOD OLD PLANET EARTH FOREVER.

IN EXCHANGE FOR SOME BIOLOGICAL EXAMINATIONS, THEY ALLOWED ME TO LIVE CLANDESTINELY IN THEIR SYSTEM FOR MORE THAN 20 YEARS, UNTIL THE INTEGRATION OF OUR PLANET INTO THE CONFEDERATION.

BELIEVE ME, I'VE HAD PLENTY OF TIME TO PERFECT MY STELLAR PILOTING SKILLS!

I'LL GET YOU TO YOUR DESTINATION WITHOUT A HITCH!

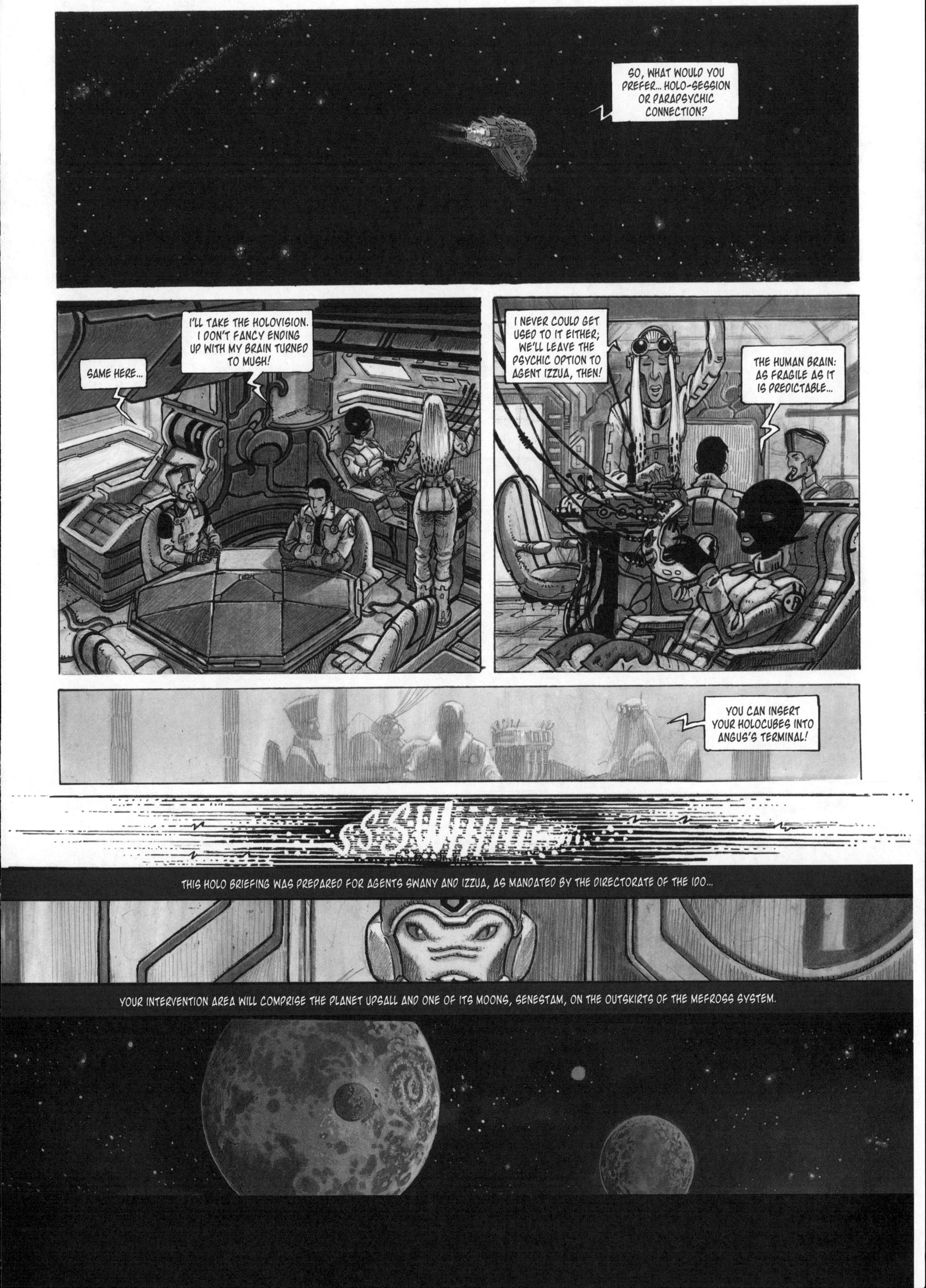
SO, WHAT WOULD YOU PREFER... HOLO-SESSION OR PARAPSYCHIC CONNECTION?
I'LL TAKE THE HOLOVISION. I DON'T FANCY ENDING UP WITH MY BRAIN TURNED TO MUSH!
SAME HERE...
I NEVER COULD GET USED TO IT EITHER; WE'LL LEAVE THE PSYCHIC OPTION TO AGENT IZZUA, THEN!
THE HUMAN BRAIN: AS FRAGILE AS IT IS PREDICTABLE...
YOU CAN INSERT YOUR HOLOCUBES INTO ANGUS'S TERMINAL!
THIS HOLO BRIEFING WAS PREPARED FOR AGENTS SWANY AND IZZUA, AS MANDATED BY THE DIRECTORATE OF THE IDO...
YOUR INTERVENTION AREA WILL COMPRISE THE PLANET UPSALL AND ONE OF ITS MOONS, SENESTAM, ON THE OUTSKIRTS OF THE MEFROSS SYSTEM.

THE GOVERNMENT OF UPSALL, REPRESENTING THE JÄVLOD PEOPLE, CONTACTED US TO FORESTALL A CONFLICT WITH A HUMAN COLONY ON SENESTAM.

THE ORIGINS OF THE CONFLICT DATE BACK TO THE REFERENDUM ON EARTH'S INTEGRATION, A TIME WHEN ISOLATIONIST VIOLENCE REACHED ITS PEAK. FRIGHTENED BY THOSE CRIMES, THE HUMANS GAVE A POSITIVE ANSWER TO CONFEDERATE INTEGRATION.

BUT TWO YEARS LATER, THE ISOLATIONISTS TOOK THE MAJORITY AT THE TERRAN GENERAL ELECTIONS. AND THE SITUATION ONCE AGAIN DETERIORATED. AS A CONFEDERACY MEMBER, THE EARTH OBTAINED ACCESS TO OUR TECHNOLOGICAL MODELS, ALLOWING HUMAN CREWS TO TRAVEL OVER VERY LONG INTERSTELLAR DISTANCES.

THE ISOLATIONIST FORCES BEGAN TO EXPLOIT PLANETARY ZONES LOCATED IN THE SANDJARR PERIMETER SO AS TO INCREASE THEIR ENERGETIC INDEPENDENCE... THEIR MILITARY MINING TEAMS ESTABLISHED THEMSELVES THERE COMPLETELY ILLEGALLY.

THE SANDJARRS QUICKLY LODGED A COMPLAINT WITH THE CONFEDERATE COUNCIL, WHO DEMANDED THAT THE TERRAN AUTHORITIES WITHDRAW THEIR TROOPS FROM THE AREAS IN QUESTION—IN VAIN.

HUMAN FORCES ATTACKED THE SANDJARR CITIES LOCATED NEAR THE EXPLOITATION ZONES, CONVINCED THAT THE PACIFISM ADVOCATED BY THE CONFEDERATION WOULD PROTECT THEM FROM A COUNTER-STRIKE.
THESE PERFIDIOUS ATTACKS KILLED TENS OF THOUSANDS OF SANDJARRS, BRINGING THEM CLOSE TO EXTINCTION.

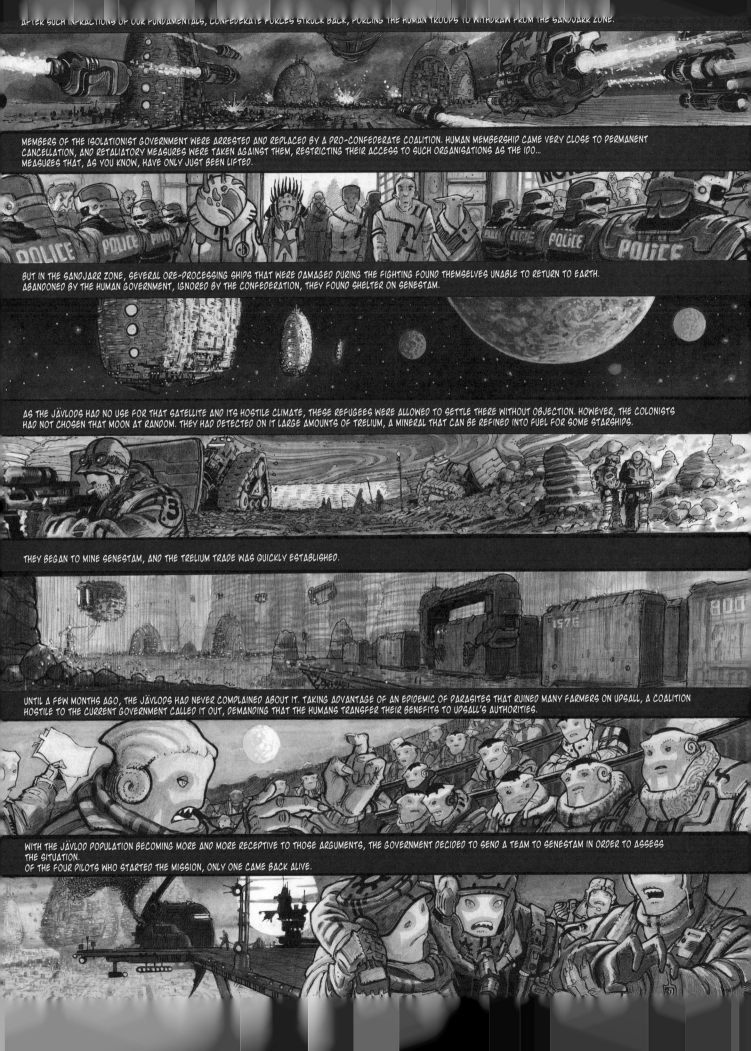

AFTER SUCH INFRACTIONS OF OUR FUNDAMENTALS, CONFEDERATE FORCES STRUCK BACK, FORCING THE HUMAN TROOPS TO WITHDRAW FROM THE SANDJARR ZONE.

MEMBERS OF THE ISOLATIONIST GOVERNMENT WERE ARRESTED AND REPLACED BY A PRO-CONFEDERATE COALITION. HUMAN MEMBERSHIP CAME VERY CLOSE TO PERMANENT CANCELLATION, AND RETALIATORY MEASURES WERE TAKEN AGAINST THEM, RESTRICTING THEIR ACCESS TO SUCH ORGANISATIONS AS THE IDO...
MEASURES THAT, AS YOU KNOW, HAVE ONLY JUST BEEN LIFTED.

BUT IN THE SANDJARR ZONE, SEVERAL ORE-PROCESSING SHIPS THAT WERE DAMAGED DURING THE FIGHTING FOUND THEMSELVES UNABLE TO RETURN TO EARTH. ABANDONED BY THE HUMAN GOVERNMENT, IGNORED BY THE CONFEDERATION, THEY FOUND SHELTER ON SENESTAM.

AS THE JÄVLODS HAD NO USE FOR THAT SATELLITE AND ITS HOSTILE CLIMATE, THESE REFUGEES WERE ALLOWED TO SETTLE THERE WITHOUT OBJECTION. HOWEVER, THE COLONISTS HAD NOT CHOSEN THAT MOON AT RANDOM. THEY HAD DETECTED ON IT LARGE AMOUNTS OF TRELIUM, A MINERAL THAT CAN BE REFINED INTO FUEL FOR SOME STARSHIPS.

THEY BEGAN TO MINE SENESTAM, AND THE TRELIUM TRADE WAS QUICKLY ESTABLISHED.

UNTIL A FEW MONTHS AGO, THE JÄVLODS HAD NEVER COMPLAINED ABOUT IT. TAKING ADVANTAGE OF AN EPIDEMIC OF PARASITES THAT RUINED MANY FARMERS ON UPSALL, A COALITION HOSTILE TO THE CURRENT GOVERNMENT CALLED IT OUT, DEMANDING THAT THE HUMANS TRANSFER THEIR BENEFITS TO UPSALL'S AUTHORITIES.

WITH THE JÄVLOD POPULATION BECOMING MORE AND MORE RECEPTIVE TO THOSE ARGUMENTS, THE GOVERNMENT DECIDED TO SEND A TEAM TO SENESTAM IN ORDER TO ASSESS THE SITUATION.
OF THE FOUR PILOTS WHO STARTED THE MISSION, ONLY ONE CAME BACK ALIVE.

SINCE THEN, THE JAVLOD OPPOSITION HAS BEEN ACCUSING THE HUMANS ON SENESTAM OF MURDERING THOSE PILOTS, WHILE THE COLONISTS CLAIM IT WAS AN ACCIDENT DUE TO A MINING-RELATED EXPLOSION.

YOU HAVE TWO OBJECTIVES: FIND OUT WHAT HAPPENED TO THOSE PILOTS AND HELP FIND A COMPROMISE BETWEEN THE JÄVLODS AND THE HUMAN COLONISTS. SEVERAL HUMAN-COMPATIBLE PLANETS ARE WILLING TO RECEIVE THEM, SO THERE ARE GOOD CHANCES OF AVOIDING A CONFLICT. WE WILL KEEP YOU INFORMED IN REAL TIME OF THE STATUS OF THE TRANSACTIONS ON THAT MATTER.

GOOD LUCK IN ACCOMPLISHING YOUR TASK. HOLO-SESSION COMPLETED.

WELL, NOW WE KNOW.

I HAVE TO GO CONFIGURE ANGUS SO HE CAN TAKE US TO THE MEFROSS SYSTEM.

I DON'T UNDERSTAND THE DIRECTORATE'S DECISION: WHY SEND A SANDJARR ON SUCH A MISSION?!

THE COLONISTS WILL TAKE IT AS A PROVOCATION!

I WOULD SAY IT'S ABOUT PROVING THAT CONFEDERATE FUNDAMENTALS ARE ABOVE ALL LOCAL ANTAGONISM.

BUT I AGREE WITH YOU ON ONE POINT...

THIS FIRST MISSION LOOKS LIKE A REAL BAPTISM BY FIRE!

34

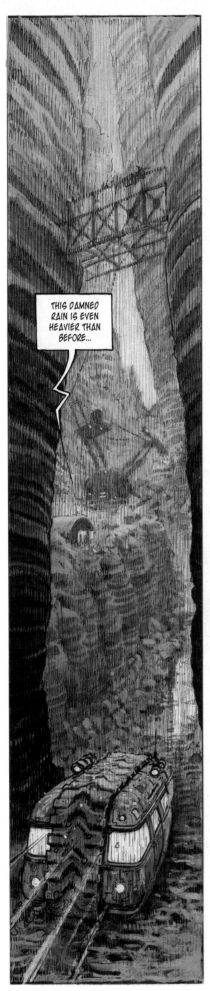

BUT THAT'S ALL THE CHARM OF SENESTAM, ISN'T IT? ANYWAY, MOST OF THE HEAVY WORK WILL BE FINISHED SOON, JOSH...

ONLY A FEW MORE ROCKS, AND THE EXTRACTORS WILL HAVE ACCESS TO THE TRELIUM!

THIS DAMNED RAIN IS EVEN HEAVIER THAN BEFORE...

!?

BRRRRRRRRRR

WHAT THE...?

A MUDSLIDE! GET CLEAR! GET CLEAR!

SHIT!!!

BRROOOOOO

35

JORAN AND LOWIE ARE STUCK INSIDE THE LIFT!

LISTEN! THEY'RE ALIVE!

BRING THE LASER DRILL! AND HAVE A VEHICLE READY TO TAKE THEM TO SHIREBRUK! QUICK!

IT'S THE FOURTH TIME IN TWO MONTHS... SHIT!

HAAAA...

HANG ON, BOYS, WE'LL TAKE GOOD CARE OF YOU.

GREGOR, I JUST GOT A MESSAGE FROM THE SPACEPORT.

HMMMM....

AGENTS SENT BY THE IDO ARE ON FINAL APPROACH... THEY WANT TO MEET WITH YOU...

IT'S ABOUT THE JÄVLODS.

LOOK AT THESE BRAVE CONFEDERATE DELEGATES...

HA HA HA HA HA

TO COME SPLASH THROUGH SENESTAM'S MUD IN THEIR SHINY NEW SUITS—NOW THAT'S COURAGE!

HELLO, I'M KIM VANDERSEEL!

I'VE BEEN ASKED TO BRING YOU TO THE COLONY'S COUNCIL...

VERY KIND OF THEM!

OUR TECHNICIANS WILL TAKE CARE OF YOUR SHUTTLE, WHICH WILL REMAIN HERE SHELTERED FROM THE WEATHER...

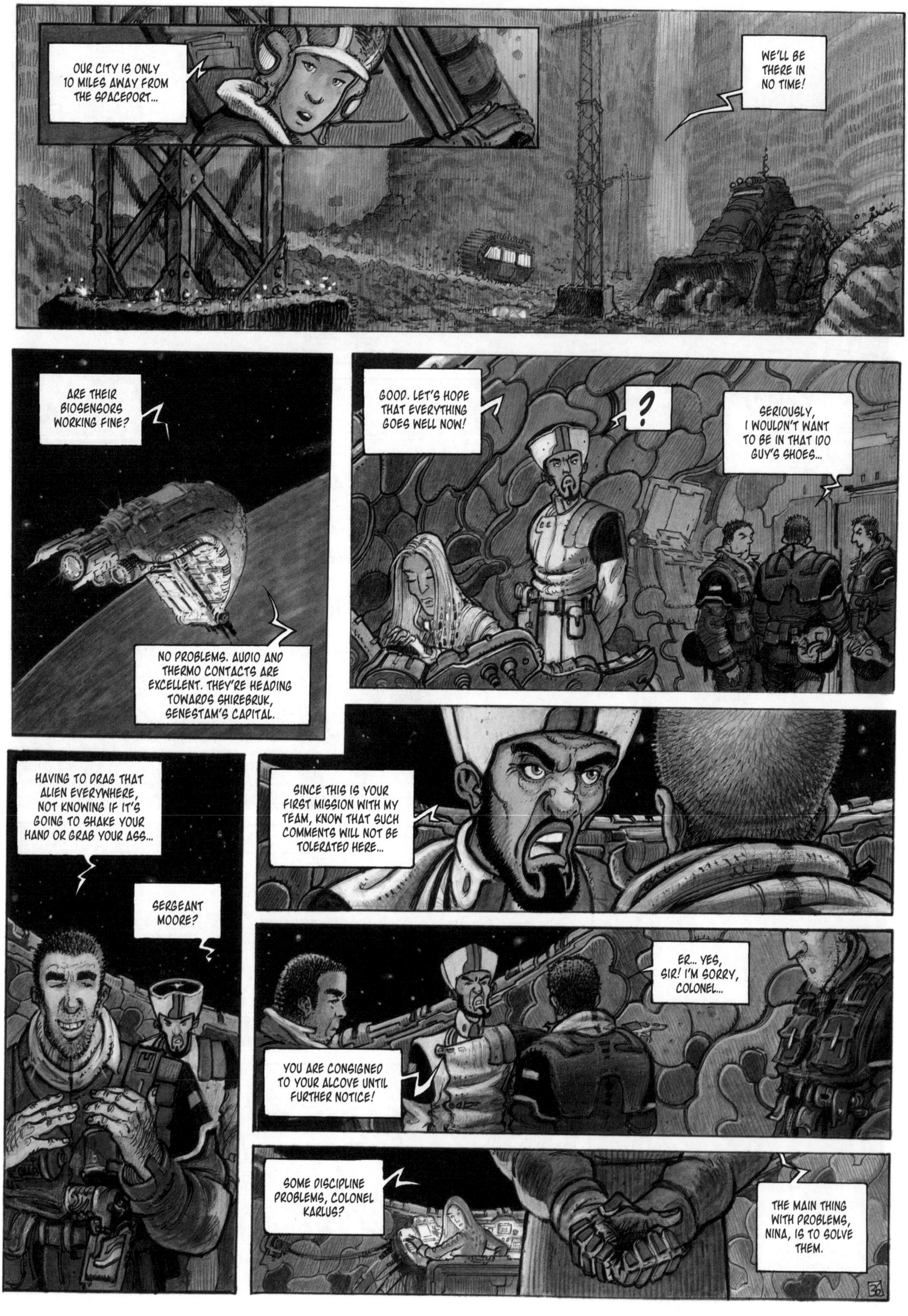
OUR CITY IS ONLY 10 MILES AWAY FROM THE SPACEPORT...
WE'LL BE THERE IN NO TIME!
ARE THEIR BIOSENSORS WORKING FINE?
NO PROBLEMS. AUDIO AND THERMO CONTACTS ARE EXCELLENT. THEY'RE HEADING TOWARDS SHIREBRUK, SENESTAM'S CAPITAL.
GOOD. LET'S HOPE THAT EVERYTHING GOES WELL NOW!
?
SERIOUSLY, I WOULDN'T WANT TO BE IN THAT IDO GUY'S SHOES...
HAVING TO DRAG THAT ALIEN EVERYWHERE, NOT KNOWING IF IT'S GOING TO SHAKE YOUR HAND OR GRAB YOUR ASS...
SERGEANT MOORE?
SINCE THIS IS YOUR FIRST MISSION WITH MY TEAM, KNOW THAT SUCH COMMENTS WILL NOT BE TOLERATED HERE...
ER... YES, SIR! I'M SORRY, COLONEL...
YOU ARE CONSIGNED TO YOUR ALCOVE UNTIL FURTHER NOTICE!
SOME DISCIPLINE PROBLEMS, COLONEL KARLUS?
THE MAIN THING WITH PROBLEMS, NINA, IS TO SOLVE THEM.
36

WE'VE REACHED THE OUTSKIRTS OF SHIREBRUK...

THIS IS WHERE OUR TRELIUM REFINERIES ARE CONCENTRATED...

ONCE TREATED, THE ORE IS STOCKED IN WAREHOUSES LOCATED NEAR THE SPACEPORT, WHERE OUR CLIENTS' CARGO SHIPS CAN COME AND LOAD IT UP...

WHAT ABOUT YOU, KIM? DO YOU ALSO WORK IN TRELIUM?

IN A WAY. SINCE I'M TRAINED AS A MICROSURGEON, I'VE BEEN PUT IN CHARGE OF SHIREBRUK'S MEDICENTRE...

AND WHEN YOU LOOK AT THE NUMBER OF ACCIDENTS LINKED TO MINING ACTIVITIES...

YOU COULD SAY I WORK IN THAT SECTOR!

39

MY FRIENDS, SEE HOW MUNLLASH SEEMS TO COME ALIVE AS IT TAKES IN THE FULL MEASURE OF THE CHANGES THAT ARE COMING...

NEVER HAS OUR CAPITAL APPEARED SO RADIANT TO MY EYES!

HEARING THE CLAMOUR OF OUR SUPPORTERS SURROUNDING THE PARLIAMENT ONLY SERVES TO REINFORCE THAT SHINE...

THE ROUND ANGER IS CONSTANTLY GAINING IN STRENGTH: THE SENESCHAL OF MY'RALL COUNTY HAS JUST JOINED OUR MOVEMENT IN HIS PROVINCE'S NAME...

WITH A FEW MORE OF UPSALL'S SENESCHALS DECLARING THEIR ALLEGIANCE TO US, WE WILL HAVE A MAJORITY!

BELIEVE ME, THE JÄVLOD PEOPLE WILL THANK US FOR GIVING THEM BACK WHAT IS RIGHTFULLY THEIRS...

SCHWIGO MORRS AND HIS LOT WILL HAVE NO OTHER CHOICE LEFT BUT TO CRAWL AT OUR FEET AND BEG FOR MERCY!

SENESCHAL WOOL, I'VE BEEN INFORMED THAT THERE IS A CLASS 1 HOLO-CALL WAITING FOR YOU IN YOUR APARTMENTS...

WELL, WELL...

MIGHT THERE BE SOME NEWS FROM ORBITAL THEN?

THANK YOU FOR ANSWERING MY CALL SO QUICKLY, SENZER WOOL!

EKKLHID, THE TIES THAT BIND MY PEOPLE TO THE ACHERODES DEMAND SWIFTNESS.

AND WHAT I HAVE TO TELL YOU WILL ONLY CONFIRM THAT...

WE HAVE JUST LEARNED THAT THE DIRECTORATE HAS DECIDED TO INTERVENE IN THE BUSINESS THAT CONCERNS US, AT THE REQUEST OF YOUR PRIME SENESCHAL SCHWIGO MORRS!

EVONA TOOT HAS JUST MANDATED TWO DIPLOMATIC AGENTS TO FIND A PEACEFUL RESOLUTION TO THE DISPUTE...

AND WHEN ARE THOSE AGENTS GOING TO ARRIVE HERE?

THEY'RE ALREADY ON SENESTAM, AND ONE OF THEM SHOULD SOON COME TO UPPSAL TO MEET WITH SENESCHAL MORRS...

THOSE VERMIN DIDN'T WASTE ANY TIME!

41

ACTUALLY, WE THINK THAT THE IDO'S INTERVENTION COULD BE A BLESSING IF WE USE IT WELL...

SENESTAM'S COLONISTS ARE UNLIKELY TO PROVE VERY ACCOMMODATING TOWARDS THEM, AND THE FAILURE OF SUCH A DIPLOMATIC MISSION COULD ACCELERATE THE CHANGE WE ARE WORKING TO BRING ABOUT...

SO, STAY ON YOUR GUARD BUT BE CONFIDENT...

I REMAIN CONVINCED WE ARE CLOSE TO VICTORY!

THEY'RE COMING, GREGOR...

I'VE SEEN.

DO WE SHOOT THEM NOW OR SHOULD WE WAIT UNTIL THEY GET INSIDE THE COUNCIL BUILDING?

COME ON, MARTUS, LOWER YOUR WEAPON...

WE SHOULD LET GREGOR TRY TO CONVINCE THEM WE'RE WITHIN OUR RIGHTS FIRST!

42

AREN'T YOU COMING WITH US, KIM?

SINCE THEY ARE HUMAN, I WILL LET YOU DO THE TALKING.

I KNOW THE PROTOCOL, AGENT IZZUA...

I WOULD HAVE LIKED TO, BUT I MUST GO TO THE MEDICENTRE...

TWO OF OUR MINERS WERE GRAVELY INJURED IN A LANDSLIDE AND I HAVE TO TAKE CARE OF THEM! I'LL JOIN YOU AS SOON AS POSSIBLE!

GREGOR VANDERSEEL, ELECTED LEADER OF SENESTAM'S COUNCIL...

DIPLOMATIC AGENTS SWANY AND IZZUA, REPRESENTING THE IDO DIRECTORATE...

IF YOU WOULD FOLLOW ME, THE REST OF THE COUNCIL IS WAITING FOR US INSIDE...

GREGOR VANDERSEEL? IF ONLY WE COULD HAVE PURSUED THE NEGOTIATIONS WITH HIS WIFE...

ERM...

SINCE THE FULL COUNCIL IS PRESENT, I'LL LET YOU EXPLAIN WHY YOU'RE HERE...

WE THANK YOU FOR YOUR ATTENTION!

THE UPSALL GOVERNMENT HAS ASKED US TO INVESTIGATE THE DEATH ON SENESTAM OF THREE OF THEIR PILOTS...

YOU ALSO KNOW THAT SINCE YOUR SETTLEMENT ON THIS MOON WAS NEVER OFFICIALLY AUTHORIZED BY THE JÄVLOO AUTHORITIES, IT IS THEIR RIGHT TO DEMAND YOUR DEPARTURE...

TO START WITH, WE HAVE AN OPENING OFFER TO MAKE YOU ON THIS SUBJECT...

GO AHEAD, ACTIVATE THE SONIC JAMMER...

HERE WE GO!

THE IDO HAS ALREADY OBTAINED AGREEMENTS FROM FIVE HUMAN-COMPATIBLE PLANETS THAT ARE WILLING TO TAKE YOU IN, THUS OFFERING YOU MUCH BETTER LIVING CONDITIONS THAN...?

DON'T BOTHER SAYING ANY MORE, AGENT SWANY.

BEFORE YOU CAME, THE JÄVLOOS CARED NOTHING FOR THIS MOON AND ITS RESERVES OF TRELIUM!

HUNDREDS OF OUR PEOPLE HAVE DIED IN THESE MINES, AND WITHOUT OUR STUBBORN DETERMINATION, NOT ONE GRAM OF ORE WOULD HAVE BEEN EXTRACTED FROM THIS GROUND, SO UNDERSTAND THIS VERY CLEARLY...

WE WILL NEVER LEAVE THIS PLACE!

WHY DON'T YOU LISTEN TO ALL OF OUR PROPOSITIONS FIRST, COUNCILLOR VANDERSEEL? THEN...

YOU'RE THE ONE WHO'S GONNA LISTEN! YOU CAN TELL YOUR ALIENS TO GO TO HELL!

I HAVE STATIC ON THE AUDIO CHANNELS...

THAT'S STRANGE...

IT'S AS IF SOMETHING DOWN THERE WAS INTERFERING WITH OUR TRANSMISSIONS!?

AND YOU DARE SHOW YOUR FACE HERE WITH ONE OF THOSE SANDJARRS AFTER WE FOUGHT AGAINST THE SCUM? I SHOULD SHOOT YOU DOWN WHERE YOU STAND!

I ADVISE YOU NOT TO COME ANY CLOSER!

PLEASE, LET US RESUME THE NEGOTIATIONS. YOU HAVE NOTHING TO GAIN BY LETTING THINGS TURN UGLY...

CLIC

GREGOR?! WHY SHOULD WE TALK WITH SO-CALLED DIPLOMATS WHEN THEY ARE OPENLY THREATENING US?

I THINK COUNCILLOR BEGGLER IS RIGHT...

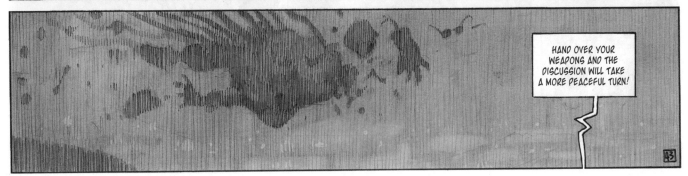

HAND OVER YOUR WEAPONS AND THE DISCUSSION WILL TAKE A MORE PEACEFUL TURN!

THAT'S OUT OF THE QUESTION! YOU KNOW WE'RE AUTHORIZED TO CARRY SUCH WEAPONS!

BRROOOOOOO

?

POW

MEZOKE, THIS ONE'S FOR US!

I'VE SEEN IT!

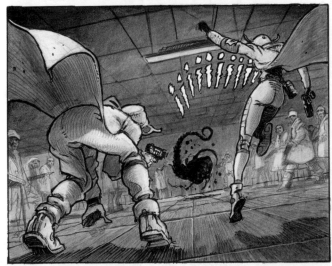

COULD YOU EXPLAIN THIS TO US, COUNCILLOR VANDERSEEL?

THESE... THESE ARE STILVULLS...

CALL THE MEDICENTRE! THEY HAVE TO TAKE CARE OF THE WOUNDED!

THESE DAMN THINGS WERE EVERYWHERE WHEN WE ARRIVED, AND IT TOOK US SEVERAL MONTHS TO EXTERMINATE THEM NEST BY NEST.

WE THOUGHT WE WERE RID OF THEM, BUT...

GREGOR, WE AREN'T DONE WITH THESE TWO!

WE HAVE TO CONFISCATE THEIR WEAPONS!

I THINK THEY JUST DEMONSTRATED THE OPPOSITE TO US, JOSH!

HELP!

OUTSIDE, WE NEED HELP!

WILLY, TAKE CARE OF HIM! EVERYONE ELSE WITH ME!

47

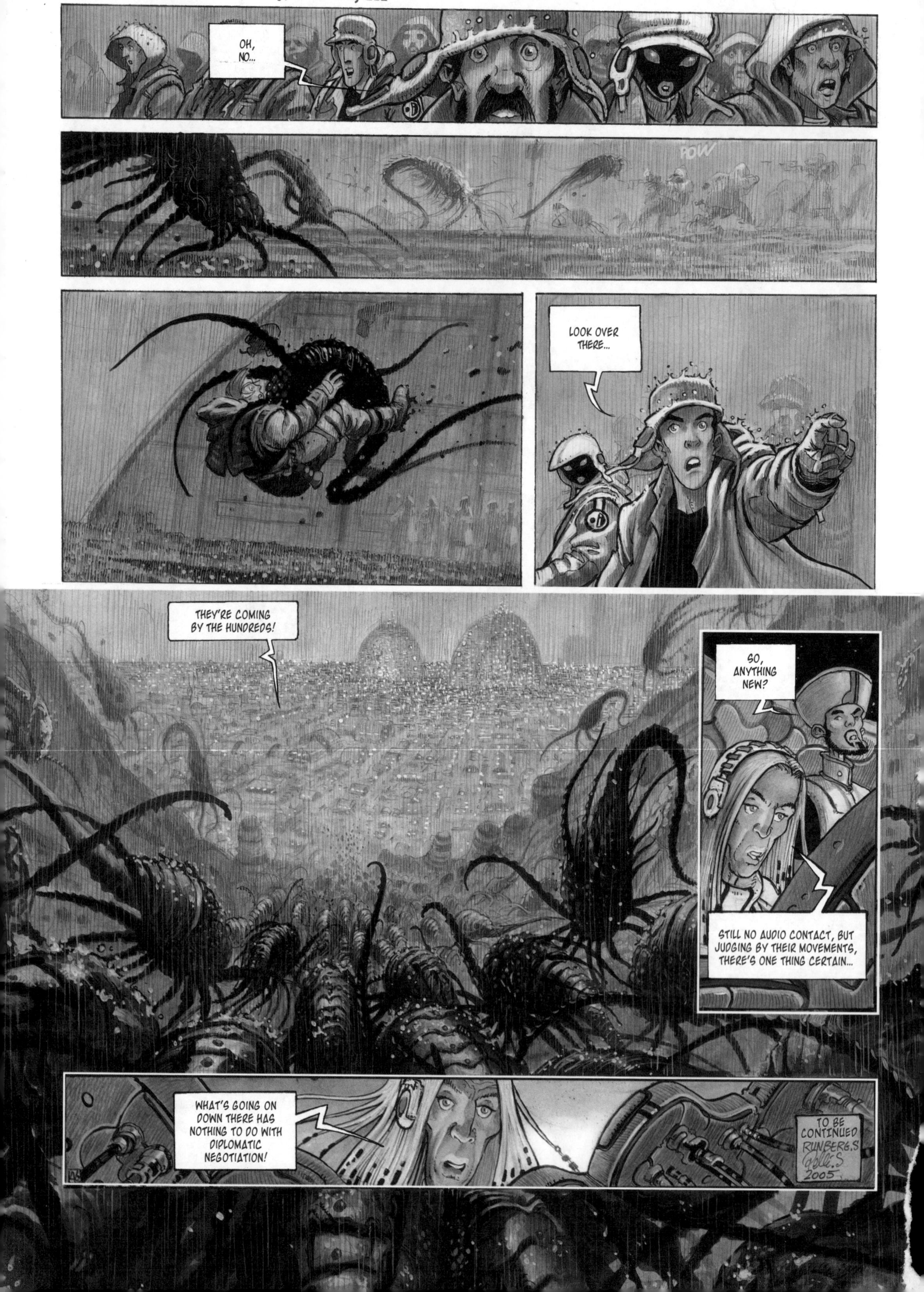
OH, NO...
POW
LOOK OVER THERE...
THEY'RE COMING BY THE HUNDREDS!
SO, ANYTHING NEW?
STILL NO AUDIO CONTACT, BUT JUDGING BY THEIR MOVEMENTS, THERE'S ONE THING CERTAIN...
WHAT'S GOING ON DOWN THERE HAS NOTHING TO DO WITH DIPLOMATIC NEGOTIATION!
TO BE CONTINUED
RUNBERG.S
2005